CLINTON TOWNSHIP
PUBLIC LIBRARY
110 S. Elm St., Box 299
Waterman, IL 60556

FOR JOSEPH AND DAVID
—SA

TO THE WESTERN ADDITION LIBRARY IN SF
WHERE, AS A NEW MOTHER AND IMMIGRANT,
I FOUND MY FIRST HOME IN THE USA. NANCY,
I HOPE YOU REMEMBER ME. YOU CHANGED MY LIFE
FOREVER WHEN YOU PUT BOOKS IN MY HANDS.
—YM

The illustrations for Thunder Boy Jr. were made from the remains of an antique house in Xalapa, Mexico, where Yuyi now has her studio and where she created this book. When the rotting roof and some of the walls came down, she picked out old wood as well as clay bricks that she later scanned and used their colors and textures to digitally paint the illustrations. This book was edited by Alvina Ling and Bethany Strout and designed by Sasha Illingworth. The production was supervised by Erika Schwartz, and the production editor was Andy Ball.

Copyright © 2016 by Sherman Alexie • Cover and Illustrations copyright © 2016 by Yuyi Morales • Cover design by Sasha Illingworth • Cover copyright © 2016 Hachette Book Group, Inc. • All rights reserved. In accordance with the U.S. Copyright Act of 1976, the scanning, uploading, and electronic sharing of any part of this book without the permission of the publisher is unlawful piracy and theft of the author's intellectual property. If you would like to use material from the book (other than for review purposes), prior written permission must be obtained by contacting the publisher at permissions@hbgusa.com. Thank you for your support of the author's rights. • Little, Brown and Company • Hachette Book Group • 1290 Avenue of the Americas, New York, NY 10104 • Visit us at lb-kids.com • Little, Brown and Company is a division of Hachette Book Group, Inc. • The Little, Brown name and logo are trademarks of Hachette Book Group, Inc. • The publisher is not responsible for websites (or their content) that are not owned by the publisher. • First Edition: May 2016 • Library of Congress Cataloging-in-Publication Data • Names: Alexie, Sherman, 1966– | Morales, Yuyi, illustrator. • Title: Thunder Boy Jr. / by Sherman Alexie ; illustrated by Yuyi Morales. • Other titles: Thunder Boy Junior • Description: First edition. | New York ; Boston : Little, Brown and Company, 2016. | Summary: "Thunder Boy Jr. wants a normal name…one that's all his own. Dad is known as Big Thunder, but Little Thunder doesn't want to share a name." —Provided by publisher. • Identifiers: LCCN 2015020263 | ISBN 9780316013727 (hardcover) • Subjects: | CYAC: Names, Personal—Fiction. | Identity—Fiction. | Indians of North America—Fiction. • Classification: LCC PZ7.A382 Th 2016 | DDC [E]—dc23 LC record available at http://lccn.loc.gov/2015020263 • APS • PRINTED IN CHINA • 10 9 8 7 6 5 4 3 2 1

THUNDER BOY JR.

BY
SHERMAN ALEXIE
ILLUSTRATED BY
YUYI MORALES

LB
LITTLE, BROWN AND COMPANY
NEW YORK BOSTON

Hello, my name is
Thunder Boy.

That's my real name.

My dad gave it to me at birth.
My mom wanted to name me Sam.

Sam is a good name.
Sam is a normal name.

THUNDER
BOY

is not a normal name.

There is nobody on earth
with the same name as me.
I am the only Thunder Boy
who has ever lived.

Or so you would think.

But I am named after my dad.
He is Thunder Boy Smith Sr.,
and I am

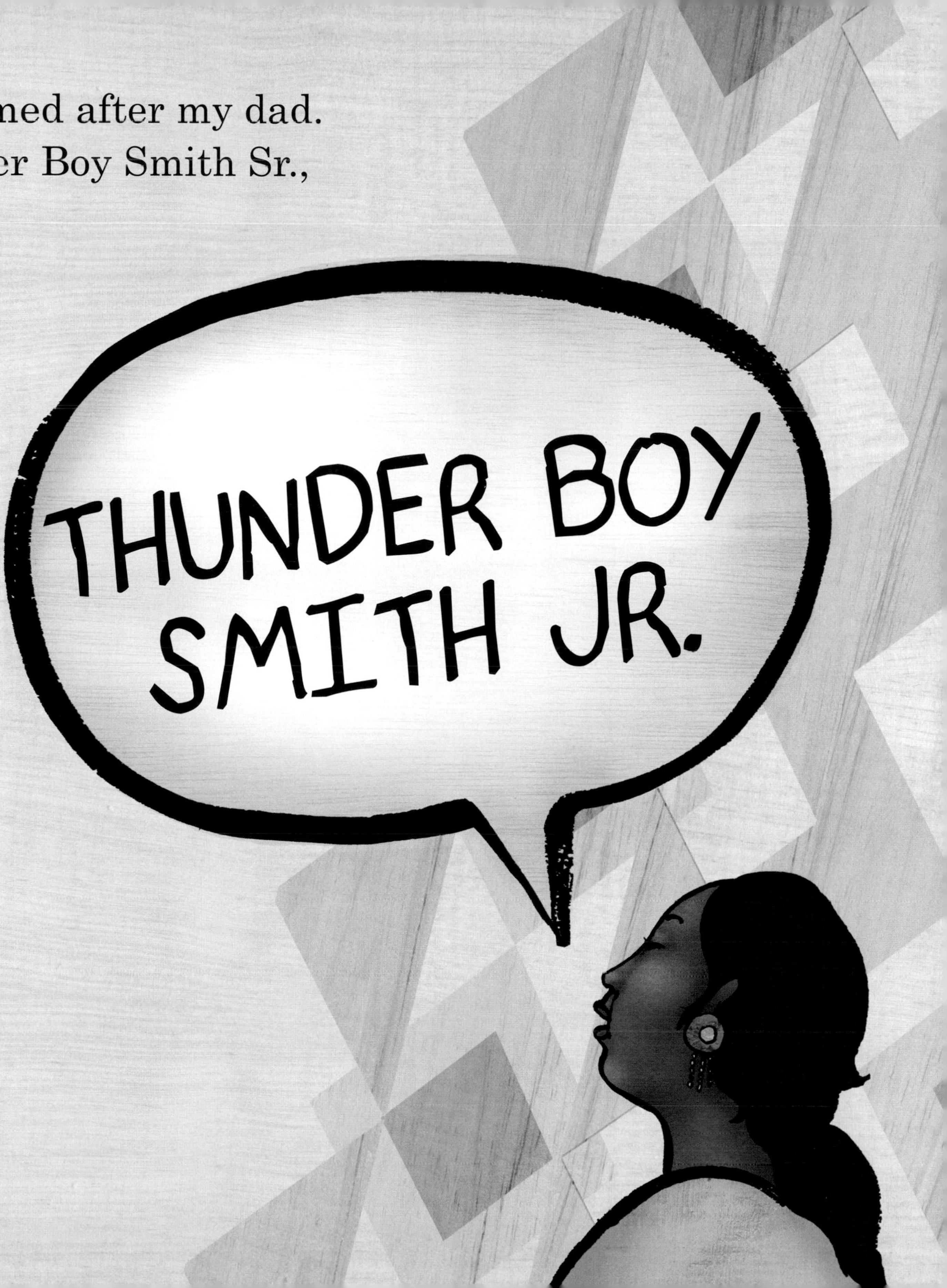

THUNDER BOY
SMITH JR.

People call him

BIG THUNDER.

That nickname is a storm filling up the sky.

People call me

That nickname makes me sound like a burp or a fart.

My mother's name is Agnes.
My sister's name is Lillian.
Those are fancy names.
But they are normal names.

Thunder Boy Jr. is not
even close to normal.

Can I tell you a secret?
Come over here
and I will whisper it in your ear.

I HATE MY NAME!

Don't get me wrong.
My dad is awesome.
But I don't want to have
the same name as him.

I WANT MY OWN NAME.

I want a name that sounds like me.
I want a name that celebrates
something cool that I've done.

CLINTON TOWNSHIP
PUBLIC LIBRARY
110 S. Elm St., Box 299
Waterman, IL 60556

I once touched a wild orca on the nose,
so maybe my name should be

NOT AFRAID
OF TEN
THOUSAND
TEETH.

I once climbed a mountain,
so maybe my name should be

I love playing in the dirt,
so maybe my name should be

MUD IN
HIS EARS.

I learned to ride a bike
when I was three,
so maybe my name should be

GRAVITY'S
BEST FRIEND.

I once dreamed the
sun and moon
were my mom and dad,
so maybe my name should be

STAR BOY.

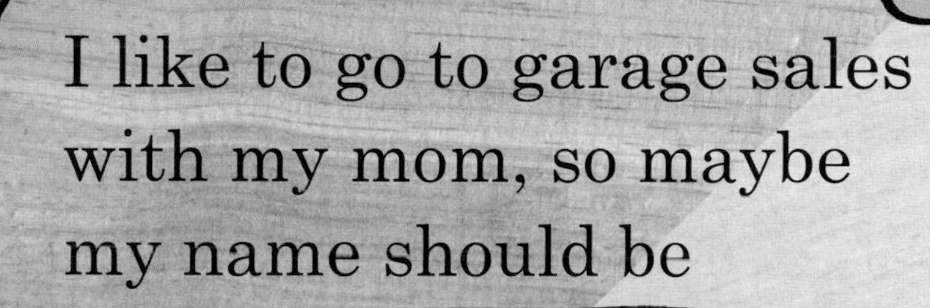

I like to go to garage sales
with my mom, so maybe
my name should be

My dog likes to chase his tail.
He likes to chase my tail.
So maybe my name should be

CAN'T RUN FAST WHILE LAUGHING.

I love powwow dancing.
I'm a grass dancer.
So maybe my name should be

I dream of traveling the world,
so maybe my name should be

FULL
OF
WONDER.

I do not want the name
they gave me when I was born.
I do not want to be

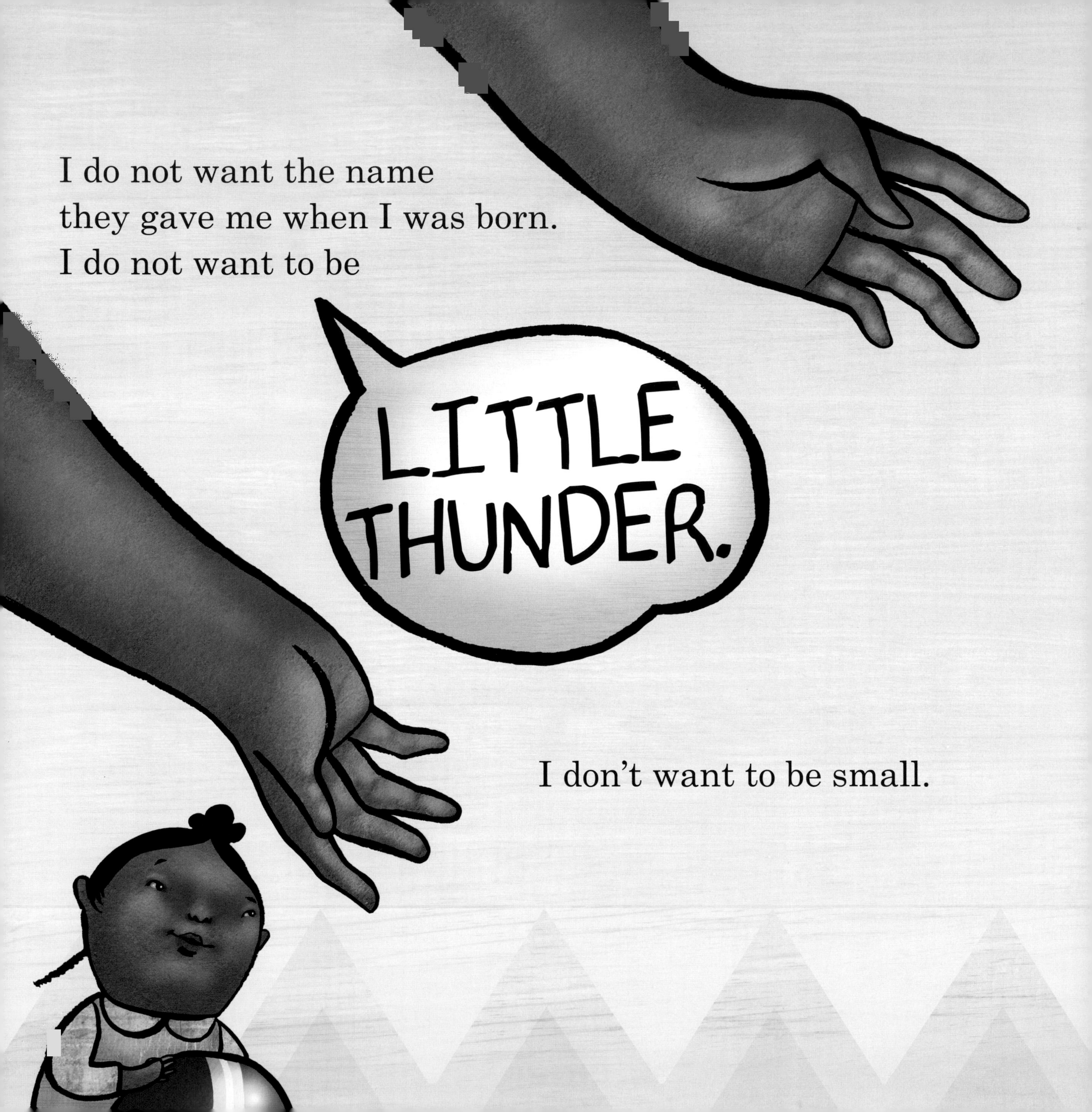

LITTLE
THUNDER.

I don't want to be small.

I love my dad but
I don't want to be exactly like him.
I love my dad but
I want to be mostly

I love my dad but
I want my own name.
What do I do?
What do I say?

“Son, I think it’s time
I gave you a new name.
A name of your own.”

My dad read my mind!
My dad read my heart!

"Son, my name will still be Thunder
but your new name will be..."

CLINTON TOWNSHIP
PUBLIC LIBRARY
110 S. Elm St., Box 299
Waterman, IL 60556

LIGHTNING!

Together, my dad and I
will become amazing weather.

Our love will be loud
and it will be bright.

My dad and I will light up the sky.